SHERL

HOLMES

in

The Bruce-Partington Plans

Sir Arthur Conan Doyle

first published in

1908

In the third week of November, in the year 1895, a dense yellow fog settled down upon London. From the Monday to the Thursday I doubt whether it was ever possible from our windows in Baker Street to see the loom of the opposite houses. The first day Holmes had spent in cross-indexing his huge book of references. The second and third had been patiently occupied upon a subject which he had recently made his hobby--the music of the Middle Ages. But when, for the fourth time, after pushing back our chairs from breakfast we saw the greasy, heavy brown swirl still drifting past us and condensing in oily drops upon the window-panes, my comrade's impatient and active nature could endure this drab existence no longer. He paced restlessly about our sitting-room in a fever of suppressed energy, biting his nails, tapping the furniture, and chafing against inaction.

"Nothing of interest

in the paper, Watson?" he said.

I was aware that by anything of interest, Holmes meant anything of criminal interest. There was the news of a revolution, of a possible war, and of an impending change of government; but these did not come within the horizon of my companion.

I could see nothing recorded in the shape of crime which was not commonplace and futile. Holmes groaned and resumed his restless meanderings.

"The London criminal is certainly a dull fellow," said he in the querulous voice of the sportsman whose game has failed him. "Look out this window, Watson. See how the figures loom up, are dimly seen, and then blend once more into the cloud-bank. The thief or the murderer could roam London on such a day as the tiger does the jungle, unseen until he pounces, and then evident only to his victim."

"There have," said

I, "been numerous petty thefts."

Holmes snorted his contempt.

"This great and sombre stage is set for something more worthy than that," said he. "It is fortunate for this community that I am not a criminal."

"It is, indeed!" said I heartily.

"Suppose that I were Brooks or Woodhouse, or any of the fifty men who have good reason for taking my life, how long could I survive against my own pursuit? A summons, a bogus appointment, and all would be over. It is well they don't have days of fog in the Latin countries--the countries of assassination. By

Jove! here comes something at last to break our dead monotony."

It was the maid with a telegram. Holmes tore it open and burst out laughing.

"Well, well! What next?" said he. "Brother Mycroft is coming round."

"Why not?" I asked.

"Why not? It is as if you met a tram-car coming down a country lane. Mycroft has his rails and he runs on them. His Pall Mall lodgings, the Diogenes Club, Whitehall--that is his cycle. Once, and only once, he has been here. What upheaval can possibly have derailed him?"

"Does he not

explain?"

Holmes handed me his brother's telegram.

"Must see you over Cadogan West. Coming at once."

MYCROFT.

"Cadogan West? I have heard the name."

"It recalls nothing to my mind. But that

Mycroft should break out in this erratic fashion! A planet might as well leave its orbit. By the way, do you know what Mycroft is?"

I had some vague recollection of an explanation at the time of the Adventure of the Greek Interpreter.

"You told me that he had some small office

under the British government."

Holmes chuckled.

"I did not know you quite so well in those days. One has to be discreet when one talks of high matters of state. You are right in thinking that he is under the British government. You would also be right in a sense if you said that occasionally he IS the British government."

"My dear Holmes!"

"I thought I might surprise you. Mycroft draws four hundred and fifty pounds a year, remains a subordinate, has no ambitions of any kind, will receive neither honour nor title, but remains the most indispensable man in the country."

"But how?"

"Well, his position is unique. He has made it for himself. There has never been anything like it before, nor will be again. He has the tidiest and most orderly brain, with the greatest capacity for storing facts, of any man living. The same great powers which

I have turned to the detection of crime he has used for this particular business. The conclusions of every department are passed to him, and he is the central exchange, the clearinghouse, which makes out the balance. All other men are specialists, but his specialism is omniscience. We will suppose that a minister needs information as to a point which involves the Navy, India, Canada and the bimetallic question; he could get his separate advices from various departments upon each, but only Mycroft can focus them all, and say offhand how each factor would affect the other. They began by using him as a short-cut, a convenience; now he has made himself an essential. In that great brain of his everything is pigeon-holed and can be handed out in an instant. Again and again his word has decided the national policy. He lives in it. He thinks of nothing else save when, as an intellectual exercise, he unbends if I call upon him and ask him to advise me on one of my little problems. But Jupiter is descending to-day. What on earth can it mean? Who is Cadogan West, and what is he to Mycroft?"

"I have it," I cried, and plunged among the litter of papers upon the sofa.

“Yes, yes, here he is, sure enough! Cadogan West was the young man who was found dead on the Underground on Tuesday morning.”

Holmes sat up at attention, his pipe halfway to his lips.

“This must be serious, Watson. A death which has caused my brother to alter his habits can be no ordinary one. What in the world can he have to do with it? The case was featureless as I remember it. The young man had apparently fallen out of the train and killed himself. He had not been robbed, and there was no particular reason to suspect violence. Is that not so?"

"There has been an inquest," said I, "and a good many fresh facts have come out. Looked at more closely, I should certainly say that it was a curious case."

"Judging by its effect upon my brother, I should think it must be a most extraordinary one." He snuggled down in his armchair. "Now,

Watson, let us have the facts."

"The man's name was Arthur Cadogan West. He was twenty-seven years of age, unmarried, and a clerk at Woolwich Arsenal."

"Government employ. Behold the link with Brother Mycroft!"

"He left Woolwich suddenly on Monday

night. Was last seen by his fiancee, Miss Violet Westbury, whom he left abruptly in the fog about 7:30 that evening. There was no quarrel between them and she can give no motive for his action. The next thing heard of him was when his dead body was discovered by a plate-layer named Mason, just outside Aldgate Station on the Underground system in London."

"When?"

"The body was found at six on Tuesday morning. It was lying wide of the metals upon the left hand of the track as one goes eastward, at a point close to the station, where the line emerges from the tunnel in which it runs. The head was badly crushed--an injury which might well have been caused by a fall from the train. The body could only have come on the line in that way. Had it been carried down from any neighbouring street, it must have passed the station barriers, where a collector is always standing. This point seems absolutely certain."

"Very good. The case is definite enough. The man, dead or alive, either fell or was precipitated from a train. So much is clear to me. Continue."

"The trains which traverse the lines of rail beside which the body was found are those which run from west to east, some being purely Metropolitan, and some from Willesden and outlying junctions. It can be stated for certain that this young man, when he met his death, was travelling in this direction at some late hour of the night, but at what point he entered the train it is impossible to state.”

“His ticket, of course, would show that.”

“There was no ticket in his pockets.”

“No ticket! Dear me, Watson, this is really very singular. According to my experience it is not possible to reach the platform of a Metropolitan train without exhibiting one's ticket. Presumably, then, the young man had one. Was it taken from him in order to conceal the station from which he came? It is possible. Or did he drop it in the carriage? That is also possible. But the point is of curious interest. I understand that there was no sign of robbery?"

"Apparently not. There is a list here of his possessions. His purse contained two pounds fifteen. He had also a check-book on the Woolwich branch of the Capital and Counties Bank. Through this his identity was established. There were also two dress-circle tickets for the Woolwich Theatre, dated for that very evening. Also a small packet of technical papers."

Holmes gave an exclamation of satisfaction.

"There we have it at last, Watson! British government--Woolwich. Arsenal--technical papers--Brother Mycroft, the chain is complete. But here he comes, if I am not mistaken, to speak for himself."

A moment later the tall and portly form of Mycroft Holmes was ushered into the room. Heavily built and massive, there was a suggestion of uncouth physical inertia in the figure, but above this unwieldy frame there was perched a head so masterful in its brow, so alert in its steel-gray, deep-set eyes, so firm in its lips, and so subtle in its play of expression, that after the first glance one forgot the gross body and remembered only the dominant mind.

At his heels came our old friend Lestrade, of

Scotland Yard--thin and austere. The gravity of both their faces foretold some weighty quest. The detective shook hands without a word. Mycroft Holmes struggled out of his overcoat and subsided into an armchair.

“A most annoying business, Sherlock,” said he. “I extremely

dislike altering my habits, but the powers that be would take no denial. In the present state of Siam it is most awkward that I should be away from the office. But it is a real crisis. I have never seen the Prime Minister so upset. As to the Admiralty--it is buzzing like an overturned bee-hive. Have you read up the case?"

"We have just done so. What were the technical papers?"

"Ah, there's the point! Fortunately, it has not come out. The press would be furious if it did. The papers which this wretched youth had in his pocket were the plans of the Bruce-Partington submarine."

Mycroft Holmes

spoke with a solemnity which showed his sense of the importance of the subject. His brother and I sat expectant.

"Surely you have heard of it? I thought everyone had heard of it."

"Only as a name."

"Its importance can hardly be

exaggerated. It has been the most jealously guarded of all government secrets. You may take it from me that naval warfare becomes impossible within the radius of a Bruce-Partington's operation. Two years ago a very large sum was smuggled through the Estimates and was expended in acquiring a monopoly of the invention. Every effort has been made to keep the secret. The plans, which are exceedingly intricate, comprising some thirty separate patents, each essential to the working of the whole, are kept in an elaborate safe in a confidential office adjoining the arsenal, with burglar-proof doors and windows. Under no conceivable circumstances were the plans to be taken from the office. If the chief constructor of the Navy desired to consult them, even he was forced to go to the Woolwich office for the purpose. And yet here we find them in the pocket of a dead junior clerk in the heart of London. From an official point of view it's simply awful."

"But you have recovered them?"

"No, Sherlock, no! That's the pinch. We have not. Ten papers were taken from Woolwich. There were seven in the pocket of Cadogan West. The three most essential are gone--stolen, vanished. You must drop everything, Sherlock. Never mind your usual petty puzzles of the police-court. It's a vital international problem that you have to solve. Why did Cadogan West take the papers, where are the missing ones, how did he die, how came his body where it was found, how can the evil be set right? Find an answer to all these questions, and you will have done good service for your country."

"Why do you not solve it yourself, Mycroft? You can see as far as I."

"Possibly, Sherlock. But it is a question of getting details. Give me your details, and from an armchair

I will return you an excellent expert opinion. But to run here and run there, to cross-question railway guards, and lie on my face with a lens to my eye--it is not my metier. No, you are the one man who can clear the matter up. If you have a fancy to see your name in the next honours list--"

My friend smiled and shook his head.

"I play the game for the game's own sake," said he. "But the problem certainly presents some points of interest, and I shall be very pleased to look into it. Some more facts, please."

"I have jotted down the more essential ones upon this sheet of paper, together with a few addresses which you will find of service. The actual official guardian of the papers is the famous government expert, Sir James Walter, whose decorations and sub-titles fill two lines of a book of reference. He has grown gray in the service, is a gentleman, a favoured guest in the most exalted houses, and, above all, a man whose patriotism is beyond suspicion. He is one of two who have a key of the safe. I may add that the papers were undoubtedly in the office during working hours on Monday, and that Sir James left for London about three o'clock taking his key with him. He was at the house of Admiral Sinclair at Barclay Square during the whole of the evening when this incident occurred."

"Has the fact been verified?"

"Yes; his brother, Colonel Valentine Walter, has testified to his departure from Woolwich, and Admiral Sinclair to his arrival in London;

so Sir James is no longer a direct factor in the problem."

"Who was the other man with a key?"

"The senior clerk and draughtsman, Mr. Sidney Johnson. He is a man of forty, married, with five children. He is a silent, morose man, but he has, on the whole, an excellent record in the public service. He is unpopular with his colleagues, but a hard worker. According to his own account, corroborated only by the word of his wife, he was at home the whole of Monday evening after office hours, and his key has never left the watch-chain upon which it hangs."

"Tell us about Cadogan West."

"He has been ten years in the service and has done good work. He has the reputation of being hot-headed and imperious, but a straight, honest man. We have nothing against him. He was next Sidney Johnson in the office. His duties brought him into daily, personal contact with the plans. No one else had the handling of them."

"Who locked up the plans that night?"

"Mr. Sidney Johnson, the senior clerk."

"Well, it is surely perfectly clear who took them away. They are actually found upon the person of this junior clerk, Cadogan West. That seems final, does it not?"

"It does, Sherlock, and yet it leaves so much unexplained. In the first place, why did he take them?"

"I presume they were of value?"

"He could have got several thousands for them very easily."

"Can you suggest any possible motive for taking the papers to London except to sell them?"

"No, I cannot."

"Then we must take that as our working hypothesis. Young West took the papers. Now this could only be done by having a false key--"

"Several false keys. He had to open the building and the room."

"He had, then, several false keys. He took the papers to London to sell the secret, intending, no doubt, to have the plans themselves back in the safe next morning before they were missed. While in London on this treasonable mission he met his end."

"How?"

"We will suppose that he was travelling back to Woolwich when he was killed and thrown out of the compartment."

"Aldgate, where the body was found, is considerably past the station London

Bridge, which would be his route to Woolwich."

"Many circumstances could be imagined under which he would pass London Bridge. There was someone in the carriage, for example, with whom he was having an absorbing interview. This interview led to a violent scene in which he lost his life.

Possibly he tried to leave the carriage, fell out on the line, and so met his end. The other closed the door. There was a thick fog, and nothing could be seen."

"No better explanation can be given with our present knowledge; and yet consider, Sherlock, how much you leave untouched. We will suppose, for argument's sake, that young Cadogan West HAD determined to convey these papers to London. He would naturally have made an appointment with the foreign agent and kept his evening clear. Instead of that he took two tickets for the theatre, escorted his fiancee halfway there, and then suddenly disappeared."

"A blind," said Lestrade, who had sat listening with some impatience to the conversation.

"A very singular one. That is objection No. 1. Objection No. 2: We will suppose that he reaches London and sees the foreign agent. He must bring back the papers before morning or the loss will be discovered. He took away ten. Only seven were in his pocket. What had become of the other three? He certainly would not leave them of his own free will. Then, again, where is the price of his treason? Once would have expected to find a large sum of money in his pocket."

“It seems to me perfectly clear,” said Lestrade. “I have no doubt at all as to what occurred. He took the papers to sell them. He saw the agent. They could not agree as to price. He started home again, but the agent went with him. In the train the agent murdered him, took the more essential papers, and threw his body from the carriage. That would account for everything, would it not?"

"Why had he no ticket?"

"The ticket would have shown which station was nearest the agent's house. Therefore he took it from the murdered man's pocket."

"Good, Lestrade, very good," said Holmes. "Your theory holds together. But if this is true, then the case is at an end. On the one hand, the traitor is dead. On the other, the plans of the Bruce-Partington submarine are presumably already on the Continent. What is there for us to do?"

"To act, Sherlock--to act!" cried Mycroft, springing to his feet. "All my instincts are against this explanation. Use your powers! Go to the scene of the crime! See the people concerned! Leave no stone unturned! In all your career you have never had so great a chance of serving your country."

"Well, well!" said Holmes, shrugging his shoulders. "Come, Watson! And you, Lestrade, could you favour us with your company for an hour or two? We will begin our investigation by a visit to Aldgate Station. Good-bye, Mycroft. I shall let you have a report before evening, but I warn you in advance that you have little to expect."

An hour later Holmes, Lestrade and I stood upon the Underground railroad at the point where it emerges from the tunnel immediately before Aldgate Station. A courteous red-faced old gentleman represented the railway company.

"This is where

the young man's body lay," said he, indicating a spot about three feet from the metals. "It could not have fallen from above, for these, as you see, are all blank walls. Therefore, it could only have come from a train, and that train, so far as we can trace it, must have passed about midnight on Monday."

"Have the carriages been examined for any sign of violence?"

"There are no such signs, and no ticket has been found."

"No record of a door being found open?"

"None."

"We have had some fresh evidence this morning,"

said Lestrade. "A passenger who passed Aldgate in an ordinary Metropolitan train about 11:40 on Monday night declares that he heard a heavy thud, as of a body striking the line, just before the train reached the station. There was dense fog, however, and nothing could be seen. He made no report of it at the time. Why, whatever is the matter with Mr. Holmes?"

My friend was standing with an expression of strained intensity upon his face, staring at the railway metals where they curved out of the tunnel. Aldgate is a junction, and there was a network of points. On these his eager, questioning eyes were fixed, and I saw on his keen, alert face that tightening of the lips, that quiver of the nostrils, and concentration of the heavy, tufted brows which I knew so well.

"Points," he muttered; "the points."

"What of it? What do you mean?"

"I suppose there are no great number of points on a system such as this?"

"No; they are very few."

"And a curve, too. Points, and a curve. By Jove! if it were only so."

"What is it, Mr. Holmes? Have you a clue?"

"An idea--an indication, no more. But the case certainly grows in interest. Unique, perfectly unique, and yet why not? I do not see any indications of bleeding on the line."

"There were hardly any."

"But I understand that there was a considerable wound."

"The bone was crushed, but there was no great external injury."

"And yet one would have expected some bleeding. Would it be possible for me to inspect the train which contained the passenger who heard the thud of a fall in the fog?"

"I fear not, Mr. Holmes. The train

has been broken up before now, and the carriages redistributed."

"I can assure you, Mr. Holmes," said Lestrade, "that every carriage has been carefully examined. I saw to it myself."

It was one of my friend's most obvious weaknesses that he was impatient with less alert intelligences than his own.

"Very likely," said he, turning away. "As it happens, it was not the carriages which I desired to examine. Watson, we have done all we can here. We need not trouble you any further, Mr. Lestrade. I think our investigations must now carry us to Woolwich."

At London Bridge, Holmes wrote a telegram to his brother, which he handed to me before dispatching it. It ran thus:

See some light in the darkness, but it may possibly flicker out. Meanwhile, please send by messenger, to await return at Baker Street, a complete list of all foreign spies or international agents known to be in England, with full address.

Sherlock.

"That should be helpful, Watson," he remarked as we took our seats in the Woolwich train. "We certainly owe Brother Mycroft a debt for having introduced us to what promises

to be a really very remarkable case."

His eager face still wore that expression of intense and high-strung energy, which showed me that some novel and suggestive circumstance had opened up a stimulating line of thought. See the foxhound with hanging ears and drooping tail as it lolls about the kennels, and compare it with the same hound as, with gleaming eyes and straining muscles, it runs upon a breast-high scent--such was the change in Holmes since the morning. He was a different man from the limp and lounging figure in the mouse-coloured dressing-gown who had prowled so restlessly only a few hours before round the fog-girt room.

“There is material here. There is scope,” said he. “I am dull indeed not to have understood its possibilities.”

“Even now they are dark to me.”

“The end is dark to

me also, but I have hold of one idea which may lead us far. The man met his death elsewhere, and his body was on the ROOF of a carriage."

"On the roof!"

"Remarkable, is it not? But consider the facts. Is it a coincidence that it is found at the very point where the train pitches and sways as it comes round on the points? Is not that the place where an object upon the roof might be expected to fall off? The points would affect no object inside the train. Either the body fell from the roof, or a very curious coincidence has occurred. But now consider the question of the blood. Of course, there was no bleeding on the line if the body had bled elsewhere. Each fact is suggestive in itself. Together they have a cumulative force."

"And the ticket, too!" I cried.

"Exactly. We could not explain the absence of a ticket. This would explain it. Everything fits together."

"But suppose it were so, we are still as far as ever from unravelling the mystery of his death. Indeed, it becomes not simpler but stranger."

"Perhaps," said Holmes, thoughtfully, "perhaps." He relapsed into a silent reverie, which lasted until the slow train drew up at last in

Woolwich Station. There he called a cab and drew Mycroft's paper from his pocket.

"We have quite a little round of afternoon calls to make," said he. "I think that Sir James Walter claims our first attention."

The house of the famous official was a fine villa with green lawns stretching down to the Thames. As we reached it the fog was lifting, and a thin, watery sunshine was breaking through. A butler answered our ring.

“Sir James, sir!” said he with solemn face. “Sir James died this morning.”

“Good heavens!” cried Holmes in amazement. “How did

he die?"

"Perhaps you would care to step in, sir, and see his brother, Colonel Valentine?"

"Yes, we had best do so."

We were ushered into a dim-lit drawing-room, where an instant later we were joined by a very tall, handsome, light-beared man of fifty, the younger brother of the dead scientist. His wild eyes, stained cheeks, and unkempt hair all spoke of the sudden blow which had fallen upon the household. He was hardly articulate as he spoke of it.

“It was this horrible scandal,” said he. “My brother, Sir James, was a man of very sensitive honour, and he could not survive such an affair. It broke his heart. He was always so proud of the efficiency of his department, and this was a crushing blow."

"We had hoped that he might have given us some indications which would have helped us to clear the matter up."

"I assure you that

it was all a mystery to him as it is to you and to all of us. He had already put all his knowledge at the disposal of the police. Naturally he had no doubt that Cadogan West was guilty. But all the rest was inconceivable."

"You cannot throw any new light upon the affair?"

"I know nothing myself save what I have read or heard. I have no desire to be discourteous, but you can understand, Mr. Holmes, that we are much disturbed at present, and I must ask you to hasten this interview to an end."

"This is indeed an unexpected development," said

my friend when we had regained the cab. "I wonder if the death was natural, or whether the poor old fellow killed himself! If the latter, may it be taken as some sign of self-reproach for duty neglected? We must leave that question to the future. Now we shall turn to the Cadogan Wests."

A small but well-kept house in the outskirts of the town sheltered the bereaved mother. The old lady was too dazed with grief to be of any use to us, but at her side was a white-faced young lady, who introduced herself as Miss Violet Westbury, the fiancee of the dead man, and the last to see him upon that fatal night.

"I cannot explain it, Mr. Holmes," she said. "I have not shut an eye since the tragedy, thinking, thinking, thinking, night and day, what the true meaning of it can be. Arthur was the most single-minded, chivalrous, patriotic man upon earth. He would have cut his right hand off before he would sell a State secret confided to his keeping. It is absurd, impossible, preposterous to anyone who knew him."

"But the facts, Miss Westbury?"

"Yes, yes; I admit I cannot explain them."

"Was he in any want

of money?"

"No; his needs were very simple and his salary ample. He had saved a few hundreds, and we were to marry at the New Year."

"No signs of any mental excitement? Come, Miss Westbury, be absolutely frank with us."

The quick eye of my companion had noted some change in her manner. She coloured and hesitated.

“Yes,” she said at last, “I had a feeling that there was something on his mind.”

“For long?”

“Only for the last week or so. He was thoughtful and

worried. Once I pressed him about it. He admitted that there was something, and that it was concerned with his official life. 'It is too serious for me to speak about, even to you,' said he. I could get nothing more."

Holmes looked grave.

"Go on, Miss Westbury. Even if it seems to tell against

him, go on. We cannot say what it may lead to."

"Indeed, I have nothing more to tell. Once or twice it seemed to me that he was on the point of telling me something. He spoke one evening of the importance of the secret, and I have some recollection that he said that no doubt foreign spies would pay a great deal to have it."

My friend's face grew graver still.

"Anything else?"

"He said that we were slack about such matters--that it would be easy for a traitor to get the plans."

"Was it only recently

that he made such remarks?"

"Yes, quite recently."

"Now tell us of that last evening."

"We were to go to the theatre. The fog was so thick that a cab was useless. We walked, and our way took us close to the office. Suddenly he darted away into the fog."

"Without a word?"

"He gave an exclamation; that was all. I waited but he never returned. Then I walked home. Next morning, after the office opened, they came to inquire. About twelve o'clock we heard the terrible news. Oh, Mr. Holmes, if you could only, only save his honour! It was so much to him."

Holmes shook his head sadly.

"Come, Watson," said he, "our ways lie elsewhere. Our next station must be the office from which the papers were taken.

"It was black enough before against this young man, but our inquiries make it blacker," he remarked as the cab lumbered off. "His coming marriage gives a motive for the crime. He naturally wanted money. The idea was in his head, since he spoke about it. He nearly made the girl an accomplice in the treason by telling her his plans. It is all very bad."

"But surely, Holmes,

character goes for something? Then, again, why should he leave the girl in the street and dart away to commit a felony?"

"Exactly! There are certainly objections. But it is a formidable case which they have to meet."

Mr. Sidney Johnson, the senior clerk, met us at the office and received us with that respect which my companion's card always commanded. He was a thin, gruff, bespectacled man of middle age, his cheeks haggard, and his hands twitching from the nervous strain to which he had been subjected.

"It is bad, Mr. Holmes, very bad! Have you heard of the death of the chief?”

“We have just come from his house.”

“The place is disorganized. The chief dead, Cadogan West dead, our papers stolen. And yet, when we closed our door on Monday evening, we were as efficient an office as any in the government service. Good God, it's dreadful to think of! That West, of all men, should have done such a thing!"

"You are sure of his guilt, then?"

"I can see no other way out of it. And yet I would have trusted him as I trust myself."

"At what hour was the office closed on Monday?"

"At five."

"Did you close it?"

"I am always the last man out."

"Where were the plans?"

"In that safe. I put them there myself."

"Is there no watchman to the building?"

"There is, but he has

other departments to look after as well. He is an old soldier and a most trustworthy man. He saw nothing that evening. Of course the fog was very thick."

"Suppose that Cadogan West wished to make his way into the building after hours; he would need three keys, would he not, before he could reach the papers?"

"Yes, he would. The key of the outer door, the key of the office, and the key of the safe."

"Only Sir James Walter and you had those keys?"

"I had no keys of the doors--only of the safe."

"Was Sir James a

man who was orderly in his habits?"

"Yes, I think he was. I know that so far as those three keys are concerned he kept them on the same ring. I have often seen them there."

"And that ring went with him to London?"

"He said so."

"And your key

never left your possession?"

"Never."

"Then West, if he is the culprit, must have had a duplicate. And yet none was found upon his body. One other point: if a clerk in this office desired to sell the plans, would it not be simpler to copy the plans for himself than to take the originals, as was actually done?"

"It would take considerable technical knowledge to copy the plans in an effective way."

"But I suppose either Sir James, or you, or West has that technical knowledge?"

"No doubt we had, but I beg you won't

try to drag me into the matter, Mr. Holmes. What is the use of our speculating in this way when the original plans were actually found on West?"

"Well, it is certainly singular that he should run the risk of taking originals if he could safely have taken copies, which would have equally served his turn."

"Singular, no doubt--and yet he did so."

"Every inquiry in this case reveals something inexplicable. Now there are three papers still missing. They are, as I understand, the vital ones."

"Yes, that is so."

"Do you mean to say that anyone holding these three papers, and without the seven others, could construct a Bruce-Partington submarine?"

"I reported to that effect to the Admiralty. But to-day I have been over the drawings again, and I am not so sure of it. The double valves with the automatic self-adjusting slots are drawn in one of the papers which have been returned. Until the foreigners had invented that for themselves they could not make the boat. Of course they might soon get over the difficulty."

"But the three missing drawings are

the most important?"

"Undoubtedly."

"I think, with your permission, I will now take a stroll round the premises. I do not recall any other question which I desired to ask."

He examined the lock of the safe, the door of the room, and finally the iron shutters of the window. It was only when we were on the lawn outside that his interest was strongly excited. There was a laurel bush outside the window, and several of the branches bore signs of having been twisted or snapped. He examined them carefully with his lens, and then some dim and vague marks upon the earth beneath. Finally he asked the chief clerk to close the iron shutters, and he pointed out to me that they hardly met in the centre, and that it would be possible for anyone outside to see what was going on within the room.

"The indications are ruined by three days' delay. They

may mean something or nothing. Well, Watson, I do not think that Woolwich can help us further. It is a small crop which we have gathered. Let us see if we can do better in London."

Yet we added one more sheaf to our harvest before we left Woolwich Station. The clerk in the ticket office was able to say with confidence that he saw Cadogan West--whom he knew well by sight--upon the Monday night, and that he went to London by the 8:15 to London Bridge. He was alone and took a single third-class ticket. The clerk was struck at the time by his excited and nervous manner. So shaky was he that he could hardly pick up his change, and the clerk had helped him with it. A reference to the timetable showed that the 8:15 was the first train which it was possible for West to take after he had left the lady about 7:30.

"Let us reconstruct, Watson," said Holmes after half an hour of silence. "I am not aware that in all our joint researches we have ever had a case which was more difficult to get at. Every fresh advance which we make only reveals a fresh ridge beyond. And yet we have surely made some appreciable progress.

“The effect of our inquiries at Woolwich has in the main

been against young Cadogan West; but the indications at the window would lend themselves to a more favourable hypothesis. Let us suppose, for example, that he had been approached by some foreign agent. It might have been done under such pledges as would have prevented him from speaking of it, and yet would have affected his thoughts in the direction indicated by his remarks to his fiancee. Very good. We will now suppose that as he went to the theatre with the young lady he suddenly, in the fog, caught a glimpse of this same agent going in the direction of the office. He was an impetuous man, quick in his decisions. Everything gave way to his duty. He followed the man, reached the window, saw the abstraction of the documents, and pursued the thief. In this way we get over the objection that no one would take originals when he could make copies. This outsider had to take originals. So far it holds together."

"What is the next step?"

"Then we come into difficulties. One would imagine that under such circumstances the first act of young Cadogan West would be to seize the villain and raise the alarm. Why did he not do so? Could it have been an official superior who took the papers? That would explain West's conduct. Or could the chief have given West the slip in the fog, and West started at once to London to head him off from his own rooms, presuming that he knew where the rooms were? The call must have been very pressing, since he left his girl standing in the fog and made no effort to communicate with her. Our scent runs cold here, and there is a vast gap between either hypothesis and the laying of West's body, with seven papers in his pocket, on the roof of a Metropolitan train. My instinct now is to work from the other end. If Mycroft has given us the list of addresses we may be able to pick our man and follow two tracks instead of one."

Surely enough, a note awaited us at Baker Street. A government messenger had brought it post-haste. Holmes glanced at it and threw it over to me.

There are numerous

small fry, but few who would handle so big an affair. The only men worth considering are Adolph Mayer, of 13 Great George Street, Westminster; Louis La Rothiere, of Campden Mansions, Notting Hill; and Hugo Oberstein, 13 Caulfield Gardens, Kensington. The latter was known to be in town on

Monday and is now reported as having left. Glad to hear you have seen some light. The Cabinet awaits your final report with the utmost anxiety. Urgent representations have arrived from the very highest quarter. The whole force of the State is at your back if you should need it.

Mycroft.

"I'm afraid," said Holmes, smiling, "that all the queen's horses and all the queen's men cannot avail in this matter." He had spread out his big map of London and leaned eagerly over it. "Well, well," said he presently with an exclamation of satisfaction, "things are turning a little in our direction at last. Why, Watson,

I do honestly believe that we are going to pull it off, after all." He slapped me on the shoulder with a sudden burst of hilarity. "I am going out now. It is only a reconnaissance. I will do nothing serious without my trusted comrade and biographer at my elbow. Do you stay here, and the odds are that you will see me again in an hour or two. If time hangs heavy get foolscap and a pen, and begin your narrative of how we saved the State."

I felt some reflection of his elation in my own mind, for I knew well that he would not depart so far from his usual austerity of demeanour unless there was good cause for exultation. All the long November evening I waited, filled with impatience for his return. At last, shortly after nine o'clock, there arrived a messenger with a note:

Am dining at Goldini's Restaurant, Gloucester Road, Kensington. Please come at once and join me there. Bring with you a jemmy, a dark lantern, a chisel, and a revolver.

S.H.

It was a nice equipment for a respectable citizen to carry through the dim, fog-draped streets. I stowed them all discreetly away in my overcoat and drove straight to the address given. There sat my friend

at a little round table near the door of the garish Italian restaurant.

"Have you had something to eat? Then join me in a coffee and curacao. Try one of the proprietor's cigars. They are less poisonous than one would expect. Have you the tools?"

"They are here, in

my overcoat."

"Excellent. Let me give you a short sketch of what I have done, with some indication of what we are about to do. Now it must be evident to you, Watson, that this young man's body was PLACED on the roof of the train. That was clear from the instant that I determined the fact that it was from the roof, and not from a carriage, that he had fallen."

"Could it not have been dropped from a bridge?"

"I should say it was impossible. If you examine the roofs you will find that they are slightly rounded, and there is no railing round them. Therefore, we can say for certain that young Cadogan West was placed on it."

"How could he be placed there?"

"That was the question which we had to answer. There is only one possible way. You are aware that the Underground runs clear of tunnels at some points in the West End. I had a vague memory that as I have travelled by it I have occasionally seen windows just above my head. Now, suppose that a train halted under such a window, would there be any difficulty in laying a body upon the roof?"

"It seems most improbable."

"We must fall back upon the old axiom

that when all other contingencies fail, whatever remains, however improbable, must be the truth. Here all other contingencies HAVE failed. When I found that the leading international agent, who had just left London, lived in a row of houses which abutted upon the Underground, I was so pleased that you were a little astonished at my sudden frivolity."

"Oh, that was it, was it?"

"Yes, that was it. Mr. Hugo Oberstein, of 13 Caulfield Gardens, had become my objective. I began my operations at Gloucester Road Station, where a very helpful official walked with me along the track and allowed me to satisfy myself not only that the back-stair windows of Caulfield Gardens open on the line but the even more essential fact that, owing to the intersection of one of the larger railways, the Underground trains are frequently held motionless for some minutes at that very spot."

"Splendid, Holmes! You have got it!"

"So far--so far, Watson. We advance, but the goal is afar. Well, having seen the back of Caulfield Gardens, I visited the front and satisfied myself that the bird was indeed flown. It is a considerable house, unfurnished, so far as I could judge, in the upper rooms. Oberstein lived there with a single valet, who was probably a confederate entirely in his confidence. We must bear in mind that Oberstein has gone to the Continent to dispose of his booty, but not with any idea of flight; for he had no reason to fear a warrant, and the idea of an amateur domiciliary visit would certainly never occur to him. Yet that is precisely what we are about to make."

"Could we not get a warrant and legalize it?"

"Hardly on the evidence."

"What can we hope to do?"

"We cannot tell what correspondence may be there."

"I don't like it, Holmes."

"My dear fellow, you shall keep watch in the street. I'll do the criminal part. It's not a time to stick at trifles. Think of Mycroft's note, of the Admiralty, the Cabinet, the exalted person who waits for news. We are bound to go."

My answer was to rise from the table.

"You are right, Holmes. We are bound to go."

He sprang up and shook me by the hand.

"I knew you would not shrink at the last," said he, and

for a moment I saw something in his eyes which was nearer to tenderness than I had ever seen. The next instant he was his masterful, practical self once more.

"It is nearly half a mile, but there is no hurry. Let us walk," said he. "Don't drop the instruments, I beg. Your arrest as a suspicious character would be a most unfortunate complication."

Caulfield Gardens was one of those lines of flat-faced pillared, and porticoed houses which are so prominent a product of the middle Victorian epoch in the West End of London. Next door there appeared to be a children's party, for the merry buzz of young voices and the clatter of a piano resounded through the night. The fog still hung about and screened us with its friendly shade. Holmes had lit his lantern and flashed it upon the massive door.

"This is a serious proposition," said

he. "It is certainly bolted as well as locked. We would do better in the area. There is an excellent archway down yonder in case a too zealous policeman should intrude. Give me a hand, Watson, and I'll do the same for you."

A minute later we were both in the area. Hardly had we

reached the dark shadows before the step of the policeman was heard in the fog above. As its soft rhythm died away, Holmes set to work upon the lower door. I saw him stoop and strain until with a sharp crash it flew open. We sprang through into the dark passage, closing the area door behind us. Holmes led the way up the curving, uncarpeted stair. His little fan of yellow light shone upon a low window.

"Here we are, Watson--this must be the one." He threw it open, and as he did so there was a low, harsh murmur, growing steadily into a loud roar as a train dashed past us in the darkness. Holmes swept his light along the window-sill. It was thickly coated with soot from the passing engines, but the black surface was blurred and rubbed in places.

"You can see where they rested the body. Halloa, Watson! what is this? There can be no doubt that it is a blood mark." He was pointing to faint discolourations along the woodwork of the window. “Here it is on the stone of the stair also. The demonstration is complete. Let us stay here until a train stops.”

We had not long to wait. The very next train roared from the tunnel as before, but slowed in the open, and then, with a creaking of brakes, pulled up immediately beneath us. It was not four feet from the window-ledge to the roof of the carriages. Holmes softly closed the window.

"So far we are justified," said he. "What do you think of it, Watson?"

"A masterpiece. You have never risen to a

greater height."

"I cannot agree with you there. From the moment that I conceived the idea of the body being upon the roof, which surely was not a very abstruse one, all the rest was inevitable. If it were not for the grave interests involved the affair up to this point would be insignificant.

Our difficulties are still before us. But perhaps we may find something here which may help us."

We had ascended the kitchen stair and entered the suite of rooms upon the first floor. One was a dining-room, severely furnished and containing nothing of interest. A second was a bedroom, which also drew blank. The remaining room appeared more promising, and my companion settled down to a systematic examination. It was littered with books and papers, and was evidently used as a study. Swiftly and methodically Holmes turned over the contents of drawer after drawer and cupboard after cupboard, but no gleam of success came to brighten his austere face. At the end of an hour he was no further than when he started.

"The cunning dog has covered his tracks," said he. "He has left nothing to incriminate him. His dangerous correspondence has been destroyed or removed. This is our last chance."

It was a small tin cash-box which stood upon the writing-desk. Holmes pried it open with his chisel. Several rolls of paper were within, covered with figures and calculations, without any note to show to what they referred. The recurring words, "water pressure" and "pressure to the square inch" suggested some possible relation to a submarine. Holmes tossed them all impatiently aside. There only remained an envelope with some small newspaper slips inside it. He shook them out on the table, and at once I saw by his eager face that his hopes had been raised.

"What's this, Watson? Eh? What's this? Record of a series of messages in the advertisements of a paper. Daily Telegraph agony column by the print and paper. Right-hand top corner of a page. No dates--but messages arrange themselves. This must be the first:

"Hoped to hear

sooner. Terms agreed to. Write fully to address given on card.

"Pierrot.

"Next comes:

"Too complex for description. Must have full report, Stuff awaits you when goods delivered.

"Pierrot.

"Then comes:

"Matter presses. Must withdraw offer unless contract completed. Make appointment by letter. Will confirm by advertisement.

"Pierrot.

"Finally:

"Monday night after nine. Two taps. Only ourselves. Do not be so suspicious. Payment in hard cash when goods *delivered.*

"Pierrot.

"A fairly complete record, Watson! If we could only get at the man at the other end!" He sat lost in thought, tapping his fingers on the table. Finally he sprang to his feet.

"Well, perhaps it won't be so difficult, after all. There is nothing more to be done here, Watson. I think we might drive round to the offices of the Daily Telegraph, and so bring a good day's work to a conclusion."

Mycroft Holmes and Lestrade had come round by appointment after breakfast next day and Sherlock Holmes had recounted to them our proceedings of the day before. The professional shook his head over our confessed burglary.

"We can't do these things in the force, Mr. Holmes," said he. "No wonder you get results that are beyond us. But some of these days you'll go too far, and you'll find yourself and your friend in trouble."

"For England, home and beauty--eh, Watson? Martyrs on the altar of our country. But what do you think of it, Mycroft?"

"Excellent, Sherlock! Admirable! But what use will you make of it?"

Holmes picked up the Daily Telegraph which lay upon the table.

"Have you seen Pierrot's advertisement to-day?"

"What? Another one?"

"Yes, here it is:

"To-night. Same hour. Same place. Two taps. Most vitally

important. Your own safety at stake.

"Pierrot.

"By George!" cried Lestrade. "If he answers that we've got him!"

"That was my idea when I put it in. I think if you could both make it convenient to come with us about eight o'clock to Caulfield

Gardens we might possibly get a little nearer to a solution."

One of the most remarkable characteristics of Sherlock Holmes was his power of throwing his brain out of action and switching all his thoughts on to lighter things whenever he had convinced himself that he could no longer work to advantage. I remember that during the whole of that memorable day he lost himself in a monograph which he had undertaken upon the Polyphonic Motets of Lassus. For my own part I had none of this power of detachment, and the day, in consequence, appeared to be interminable. The great national importance of the issue, the suspense in high quarters, the direct nature of the experiment which we were trying--all combined to work upon my nerve. It was a relief to me when at last, after a light dinner, we set out upon our expedition. Lestrade and Mycroft met us by appointment at the outside of Gloucester Road Station. The area door of Oberstein's house had been left open the night before, and it was necessary for me, as Mycroft Holmes absolutely and indignantly declined to climb the railings, to pass in and open the hall door. By nine o'clock we were all seated in the study, waiting patiently for our man.

An hour passed and yet another. When eleven struck, the measured beat of the great church clock seemed to sound the dirge of our hopes. Lestrade and Mycroft were fidgeting in their seats and looking twice a minute at their watches. Holmes sat silent and composed, his eyelids half shut, but every sense on the alert. He raised his head with a sudden jerk.

"He is coming," said he.

There had been a furtive step past the door. Now it returned. We heard a shuffling sound outside, and then two sharp taps with the knocker. Holmes rose, motioning us to remain seated. The gas in the hall was a mere point of light. He opened the outer door, and then as a dark figure slipped past him he closed and fastened it. "This way!" we heard him say, and a moment later our man stood before us. Holmes had followed him closely, and as the man turned with a cry of surprise and alarm he caught him by the collar and threw him back into the room. Before our prisoner had recovered his balance the door was shut and Holmes standing with his back against it. The man glared round him, staggered, and fell senseless upon the floor.

With the shock, his

broad-brimmed hat flew from his head, his cravat slipped down from his lips, and there were the long light beard and the soft, handsome delicate features of Colonel Valentine Walter.

Holmes gave a whistle of surprise.

“You can write me down an ass this time, Watson,” said

he. "This was not the bird that I was looking for."

"Who is he?" asked Mycroft eagerly.

"The younger brother of the late Sir James Walter, the head of the Submarine Department. Yes, yes; I see the fall of the cards. He is coming to. I think that you had best leave his examination to me."

We had carried the prostrate body to the sofa. Now our prisoner sat up, looked round him with a horror-stricken face, and passed his hand over his forehead, like one who cannot believe his own senses.

"What is this?" he asked. "I came here to visit Mr.

Oberstein."

"Everything is known, Colonel Walter," said Holmes. "How an English gentleman could behave in such a manner is beyond my comprehension. But your whole correspondence and relations with Oberstein are within our knowledge. So also are the circumstances connected with the death of young Cadogan West. Let me advise you to gain at least the small credit for repentance and confession, since there are still some details which we can only learn from your lips."

The man groaned and sank his face in his hands. We waited,

but he was silent.

“I can assure you,” said Holmes, “that every essential is already known. We know that you were pressed for money; that you took an impress of the keys which your brother held; and that you entered into a correspondence with Oberstein, who answered your letters through the advertisement columns of the Daily Telegraph. We are aware that you went down to the office in the fog on Monday night, but that you were seen and followed by young Cadogan West, who had probably some previous reason to suspect you. He saw your theft, but could not give the alarm, as it was just possible that you were taking the papers to your brother in London. Leaving all his private concerns, like the good citizen that he was, he followed you closely in the fog and kept at your heels until you reached this very house. There he intervened, and then it was, Colonel

Walter, that to treason you added the more terrible crime of murder."

"I did not! I did not! Before God I swear that I did not!" cried our wretched prisoner.

"Tell us, then, how Cadogan West met his end before you laid him upon the roof of a railway carriage."

"I will. I swear to you that I will. I did the rest. I confess it. It was just as you say. A Stock Exchange debt had to be paid. I needed the money badly. Oberstein offered me five thousand. It was to save myself from ruin. But as to murder, I am as innocent as you."

"What happened,

then?”

“He had his suspicions before, and he followed me as you describe. I never knew it until I was at the very door. It was thick fog, and one could not see three yards. I had given two taps and Oberstein had come to the door. The young man rushed up and demanded to know what we were about to do with the papers. Oberstein had a short life-preserver. He always carried it with him. As West forced his way after us into the house Oberstein struck him on the head. The blow was a fatal one. He was dead within five minutes. There he lay in the hall, and we were at our wit's end what to do. Then Oberstein had this idea about the trains which halted under his back window. But first he examined the papers which I had brought. He said that three of them were essential, and that he must keep them. 'You cannot keep them,' said I. 'There will be a dreadful row at Woolwich if they are not returned.'

'I must keep them,' said he, 'for they are so technical that it is impossible in the time to make copies.' 'Then they must all go back together to-night,' said I. He thought for a little, and then he cried out that he had it. 'Three I will keep,' said he. 'The others we will stuff into the pocket of this young man. When he is found the whole business will assuredly be put to his account.' I could see no other way out of it, so we did as he suggested. We waited half an hour at the window before a train stopped. It was so thick that nothing could be seen, and we had no difficulty in lowering West's body on to the train. That was the end of the matter so far as I was concerned."

"And your brother?"

"He said nothing, but he had caught me once with his keys, and I think that he suspected. I read in his eyes that he suspected. As you know, he never held up his head again."

There was silence in the room. It was broken by Mycroft

Holmes.

"Can you not make reparation? It would ease your conscience, and possibly your punishment."

"What reparation can I make?"

"Where is Oberstein with the papers?"

"I do not know."

"Did he give you no

address?"

"He said that letters to the Hotel du Louvre, Paris, would eventually reach him."

"Then reparation is still within your power," said Sherlock Holmes.

"I will do anything I can. I owe this fellow no particular good-will. He has been my ruin and my downfall."

"Here are paper and pen. Sit at this desk and write to my dictation. Direct the envelope to the address given. That is right. Now the letter:

"Dear Sir:

"With regard to our transaction, you will no doubt have

observed by now that one essential detail is missing. I have a tracing which will make it complete. This has involved me in extra trouble, however, and I must ask you for a further advance of five hundred pounds. I will not trust it to the post, nor will I take anything but gold or notes. I would come to you abroad, but it would excite remark if I left the country at present. Therefore I shall expect to meet you in the smoking-room of the Charing Cross Hotel at noon on Saturday. Remember that only English notes, or gold, will be taken.

"That will do very well. I shall be very much surprised if it

does not fetch our man."

And it did! It is a matter of history--that secret history of a nation which is often so much more intimate and interesting than its public chronicles--that Oberstein, eager to complete the coup of his lifetime, came to the lure and was safely engulfed for fifteen years in a British prison. In his trunk were found the invaluable Bruce-Partington plans, which he had put up for auction in all the naval centres of Europe.

Colonel Walter died in prison towards the end of the second year of his sentence. As to Holmes, he returned refreshed to his monograph upon the Polyphonic Motets of Lassus, which has since been printed for private circulation, and is said by experts to be the last word upon the subject. Some weeks afterwards I learned incidentally that my friend spent a day at Windsor, whence he returned with a remarkably fine emerald tie-pin.

When I asked him if he had bought it, he answered that it was a present from a certain gracious lady in whose interests he had once been fortunate enough to carry out a small commission. He said no more; but I fancy that I could guess at that lady's august name, and I have little doubt that the emerald pin will forever recall to my friend's memory the adventure of the Bruce-Partington plans.

THE END

ABOUT THE AUTHOR

Sir Arthur Conan Doyle was a British writer. Originally a physician, he struggled to find a publisher for his work at first. He modelled Sherlock Holmes on his former university teacher Joseph Bell. His Holmes stories are generally considered milestones in the field of crime fiction.

ABOUT THE COVER

The image on the cover is adapted from a silhouette of Basil Rathbone as Sherlock Holmes by Rumensz and designs for a submarine from 1895.

SUPER
LARGE
PRINT

MORE BOOKS AT:

superlargeprint.com

KEEP ON READING!

The cover is adapted from silhouette of Basil Rathbone as Sherlock Holmes by Rumensz. (CC BY-SA 1.0)
This book is set in a font designed by Abelardo Gonzalez called OpenDyslexic

ISBN 9798684449147

Printed in Great Britain
by Amazon

13796031R00129